W9-CEK-492

To my husband Michael, with love KH
To Sophie, as promised, with love HC

Published by Pleasant Company Publications

For information, address: Book Editor, Pleasant Company Publications, 8400 Fairway Place, P.O. Box 620998, Middleton, Wisconsin 53562.

Visit our Web site at www.americangirl.com

Printed in Italy.
01 02 03 04 05 06 LEGO 10 9 8 7 6 5 4 3

Library of Congress Cataloging-in-Publication Data
Holabird, Katharine.
Angelina's Halloween / text by Katharine Holabird ;
illustrations by Helen Craig.
p. cm.
Summary: Halloween brings excitement and thrills for Angelina and her little sister Polly, who gives her an unexpected scare.
ISBN 1-58485-152-X
[1. Halloween—Fiction. 2. Mice—Fiction.]
I. Craig, Helen, ill. II. Title.
PZ7.H689 An 2000
[E]—dc21 00-022613

Angelina's Halloween

Story by Katharine Holabird Illustrations by Helen Craig

Angelina loved the excitement of Halloween. She loved dressing up and trick-or-treating and spent hours with her best friend, Alice, thinking about wonderful costumes. At last they decided to be dancing fireflies and drew beautiful pictures of wings and tiaras.

Angelina's little sister, Polly, wanted to join them. "Look at this," she kept saying, showing them her funny scribbles.

Mrs. Mouseling helped them make the delicate costumes, and when the wings and tiaras were done, Angelina and Alice practiced flying around and around the cottage.

Polly tried to fly too but kept crashing into Angelina's wings. "Why do you always copy me?" Angelina stamped her foot.

Polly hung her head. "I want wings," she cried.

"You're too little," explained Angelina, "but you could be something really scary."

Mrs. Mouseling found a sheet, and Angelina showed Polly how to be a spooky Halloween ghost.

On Halloween evening, Angelina and her friends played scary games, and Mrs. Mouseling made them a bubbling witches' brew and delicious goblin cookies.

When Mr. Mouseling came home with an enormous pumpkin, the two fireflies and the little ghost gave him quite a fright.

After the party, Angelina and her friends set off together with their trick-or-treat bags.

"Don't forget your sister," called Mrs. Mouseling as the little ghost trundled after them.

They raced each other to the General Store and sang a song about spiders and bats to Mrs. Thimble, who had a great collection of Halloween sweets. Then they went to scare Miss Lilly, the ballet teacher, who waved her wand and gave them each a lollipop. They were about to play a Halloween trick on old Mrs. Hodgepodge when all of a sudden…

…"BOO!"

Two red devils leaped out at them from behind an apple tree.
Angelina wasn't fooled and quickly recognized Spike and Sammy.
"We're not scared of you," she laughed.

"I'll bet you're scared of that house," teased Spike, pointing up the lane. "It's haunted."

Angelina skipped off toward the dark building and banged loudly on the door. "Trick or treat?" she called. There was no answer.

"Let's go inside," whispered Spike and Sammy.

Inside, the house was
strange and shadowy, and they tiptoed
around very slowly. "Ouch!" Alice stubbed her toe.
Angelina shivered, and then something lumpy bumped
into her. "Help!" she shrieked, and they all scrambled outside.

In the dark garden, a weird sound stopped them.
"OOOh. OOOh. OOOOooooooh."

"Watch out for witches," Alice warned everyone.

They peered all around, and then Angelina saw a ghostly shape struggling in the blackberry bushes. “It’s only Polly,” she sighed, dragging the little ghost out of the prickles. “Now stay with me,” she scolded.

After that, Angelina kept her eyes on the little ghost, and they went trick-or-treating all through the neighborhood, filling their bags with delicious candy.

As the moon rose high in the night sky, the village band began to play, and everyone came out to join the Grand Costume Parade.

The whole village was dressed up in marvelous costumes. The two fireflies seemed to float off the ground as they danced along, with the little ghost jumping beside them.

At the end of the evening, Miss Lilly proudly handed out prizes. "The two fireflies and the little ghost win a special award for Halloween dancing," she announced.

"Hurray!" shouted the ghost, leaping up and down.

"But you're Henry!" gasped Angelina. "Where's Polly?"

Angelina dashed up the street to Mrs. Thimble's General Store, but all the village shops were closed. She ran to Mrs. Hodgepodge's cottage, but nobody was home.

Then a fuzzy monster skipped by. "Have you seen a little ghost?" Angelina asked, but the monster sadly shook his head.

Angelina raced up and down through all the streets of the village...

…until at last she reached the haunted house. There she found Polly, sitting on the steps, sharing the goodies from her trick-or-treat bag with three little friends dressed as wizards.

"My tummy feels funny," Polly whimpered.

Angelina shook her head. "You shouldn't eat your sweets so fast," she said. "Anyway, you really scared me."

"Did I?" Polly smiled.

On the way home, Polly held Angelina's hand.
"Next Halloween, can I be a firefly just like you?" she asked.
"Next Halloween, I think I'll be an acrobat," said Angelina.
"Can I..." Polly began, "...be an acrobat too?"
"First I'll have to show you some of my tricks." Angelina smiled.

And the very next day, she did.

Place
Stamp
Here

American Girl™

PO BOX 620497
MIDDLETON WI 53562-0497